Vagina Business
By Honey Thomas

RED LOTUS READS.

COPYRIGHT

Vagina Business

Copyright© 2024 Honey Thomas

ISBN: 978-1-7355974-4-7

DEDICATION

For the ones who strive to unapologetically live life to the fullest.

DISCLAIMER

May trigger past or current situations.

This book is a written work of fiction. Any likeness of people, places, and situations are coincidental.

TABLE OF CONTENTS

Bated Breath

So many days, months, and years have gone by. I remain hopeful.
Today is the day I'll get a thank you. Maybe even an apology.
With bated breath, I long to hear the words, I love you.
Still nothing.

I almost flatlined, holding my breath.
~ VB

Mr. Satisfaction

Daily, Mr. Satisfaction greets you with a smile, showing all thirty-twos. Give or take one or two missing wisdom teeth. You straighten your posture and pretend not to see him, damn-near losing your sight, trying to strengthen your peripheral. He winks, and you nearly melt where you stand, like a bomb pop on a hot summer day. He chuckles, grabs his coffee before they call his name, and keeps it moving. You feel embarrassed and nervously fix your hair for the umpteenth time. You hear your name called and quickly grab your latte, bolting out the door, hoping to see if the highlight of your morning is still in the area.

You smell a hint of his cologne mixed with strong black coffee. This morning, though the sun is blinding, he steps into your view, blocking the sun. Without saying a word, he hands you a business card and tells you his private number is on the back. You cross your legs at the ankle and squeeze your thighs as tight as an usher's wig on first Sunday.

A couple of days go by, and you're nervous, but you can't stop thinking of him. It's now or never to reach out. Perhaps, set up a coffee date or something. You dial the number, and the most resounding voice says, "Yeah." You think,

What businessman answers the phone like a teenager?

You, however, continue with the call, "It's me, the woman you met at the coffee shop."

He clears his throat and apologizes for the way he answered the phone. He gives you an excuse that his last call was very trying. You inform him an apology isn't necessary and ask if this is a good time to talk. He agrees that it is, telling you your voice made his day. You both engage in small talk for a moment, and he asks to see you tonight at his house for dinner. You get more nervous than a heaux in church, but you're intrigued. You quickly belt out, "Sure," although you're far from certain. You were thinking of coffee on a Sunday morning. He's talking about dinner at his place tonight at seven.

Six-thirty rolls around, and you're in panic mode, thirsty-ish for deciding to go to a stranger's home. You rationalize that you know him, due to occasionally seeing him at the coffee shop. You reach his apartment, a bit impressed by the outward appearance. He opens the door and greets you with a hug. You melt in his embrace; he guides you and gives you a quick tour. It's dark, but you figure he's set the ambiance. Dinner was fast, the conversation was short, and the wine was plenty. He checked all the boxes for a first date—you know (handsome, smells good, had nice teeth, a successful business owner, etc.). So, you decide to let your hair down and enjoy yourself. It's been a minute.

Morning came quickly, and so did he. You look around, and he's nowhere to be found. Thankful for a spend-a-night bag in your trunk from your last encounter almost ten months ago, you quickly shower, brush your teeth, and get dressed. Hoping no one notices you, you get into your car and pull into traffic.

With thirty minutes to spare before work, you rush into the coffee shop and place your order, giving the Barista your name. Your order is up, and they call out a number while looking at you. You think nothing of it and continue to wait for your order. Again, they call a number, except the Barista motions for you this time.

You ask, "What's *52*?" The Barista and his coworkers do everything in their power not to laugh.

You're puzzled, until your date from last night comes out the back and says, "You're the 52nd date I've met here."

You drop your coffee from astonishment, and he rushes to help you. You push him away and proceed to curse him out. You threaten to out his company, swearing he's a womanizer preying on single women.

"My company?" he questions.

Another woman steps out of line and approaches you, introducing herself as *51*. You feel faint. At that moment, the store owner says, "Ma'am, he doesn't own this company. He's been the employee of the month so often that I gave him his business cards." The owner proceeds to thank him for housesitting last night.

He says, "No problem," as he hands the owner his keys back.

The embarrassment and shame overtake you; you're surrounded by people pointing and laughing at you. You want to say anything to make yourself look and feel better.

You cry out, "Last night wasn't worth it. The sex was over before it started!"

The coffee shop goes quiet as he steps in front of you, smiling, and says, "I got mine. You should have got yours."

Customers and staff erupt into laughter, leaving you feeling wounded. You realize you chose to go for a night of passion that turned cold. The lightbulb enters your mind, and you hear your conscience say, "He was looking for self-satisfaction that didn't concern you, Sis."

All this over coffee and a business card? Now I must be embarrassed at the doctor because you are risking it all for free coffee. Chile, I'm sick of you!
~ VB

No Ticky, No Tocky

"Taxi!" Emerald called out to the oncoming cars. Taxi 1234 pulled over, screeching its tires. The driver was an overweight white man smoking a cigar. Emerald entered the taxi and immediately asked the driver to put the cigar out.

"Where to, ma'am?" he asked, blowing smoke before putting the cigar out against his dashboard. With a look of disgust, she formed her lips to speak, but thought it best she kept quiet. It was the end of a busy work week for her, and she didn't need any distractions.

"Ma'am, unless you're going home with me, I suggest you give me an address as to where you're going." The driver laughed, showing the last of about ten rotten teeth.

Emerald could feel her stomach turning. She swallowed hard before speaking, "Vera's Place, in the West Loop."

Rolling her eyes, she cracked the window to rid her nose of the lingering cigar smell and other disgusting smells in the taxi. She hoped tonight was just as live as any other Friday night. She needed to relax, laugh, and dance like no one was watching.

"Long week, huh?" the driver asked, adjusting his rear-view mirror on Emerald's cleavage.

Emerald adjusted her blouse and continued looking out the window. She admired Chicago in the fall: the crisp weather, beautiful foliage, and birds preparing for the cold weather. It brought back memories of the holidays from when she was a little girl.

"We're here, pretty lady," Emerald heard the driver say with a look of expectation other than a thank you for the ride. *Loser!* Emerald scanned the QR code to pay, jumped out of the taxi, and slammed the door, refusing to look back.

Walking into Vera's Place, she put anything that happened before that moment in the back of her mind. The atmosphere was warm and inviting. Vera motioned Emerald over, taking her coat and purse and putting it in her office, a small room just behind the bar.

Vera came out and gave her a motherly hug, whispering, "I feel the tension, one Old Fashion coming up." Emerald smiled and took a seat at the end of the bar. Vera placed the drink on a napkin before Emerald and tapped the bar three times, saying, "Bottom's up."

Emerald took the most extended sip ever as she shimmied her shoulders. Vera laughed a hearty laugh and turned the music down.

Picking up the mic, she began to speak, "Welcome to Vera's Place. I'm Vera if you didn't know."

"Now you know," the faithful regulars hollered.

7

"You damn right. Don't start nothing, won't be nothing. It's been a long week, and we're about to lay our burdens down and PARTY until the sun comes up!" Vera shouts.

She turns the music up as Bad Boy/Having a Party by Luther Vandross began to play.

Emerald swayed back and forth, enjoying the music and the crowd. She scanned the room and noticed a tall, drank of cognac staring at her. Once they made eye contact, he began walking toward Emerald. That same blouse she adjusted to keep the loser taxi driver from seeing through, she readjusted so Mr. Cognac could get a glimpse of her soul.

She turned to face the bar, sipping her drink while peering through the mirrors Vera put up as a backsplash—or so she said. Everybody knew it was so she could have eyes in the back of her head and see any fool who wanted to make the wrong move.

"Hey, Frank. What are you having?" Vera asked.

"Whatever this beautiful young lady is having, and give her another one on me," he said as he kept his eyes on Emerald.

Vera glanced at Emerald, who responded with a nod. "Two Old Fashions coming up!" Vera shouted.

"Frank," Mr. Cognac said, holding his hand out towards Emerald.

"Emerald," she said as she took his hand. Frank kissed the back of her hand, still not taking his eyes off her.

"Funny, I've never seen you here before," Emerald said as she drank the remaining contents of her first drink.

"Yet I've seen you here on more than one occasion," Frank said, pulling a barstool closer to Emerald and taking a seat.

"Is this the first time you dared to step to me?" Emerald questioned.

Vera slid the two drinks towards them.

Frank raised his brow and smiled. "Dance with me, Emerald, my precious gemstone," he said as he stood from the bar stool.

Emerald was amused and therefore decided to allow Frank to entertain her further. She downed her second drink and sashayed to the dance floor. The sultry sounds of Frankie Beverly captivated the couples on the dance floor. Frank held Emerald close as he sang along with the music, "And though I do my very best, I just can't find happiness, and it's all because I can't get over you."

Doing a two-step, he spun Emerald around and dipped her. Upon bringing her back up, he went in for a kiss. Emerald put her finger on his lips and smiled, saying, "Not here." Frank danced her back to the bar where Vera had her coat and purse waiting.

While helping her put on her coat, he looked at Vera for reassurance. Vera hunched her shoulders as if to say: it's your business, your choice. Emerald bid Vera farewell and danced her way out the door.

Frank led her to his car. Opening the passenger door, he helped her inside. Frank looked around before getting into the driver's side. Emerald asked if he lived close. Frank told her he had multiple properties across the city, and they could go to his penthouse off Lake Shore Drive.

Emerald felt safe, especially since Vera knew him. She knew Vera wouldn't let anything happen to her. The ride to his penthouse was quiet, besides the low volume of music from the radio. As he got closer to his place, Frank suddenly asked several questions. "Where are you from? Where do you work? Is your family from Chicago? Do you have a man? Do you have children?"

"Slow down, playboy; we're not getting married. We're just spending a little time together," Emerald cautiously said.

Frank raised a brow, then relaxed. "My apologies. I should have gotten to know you better before bringing you into my personal space."

"Agreed," Emerald said with relief.

Once they exited Lake Shore Drive, Frank approached the front door, and a valet attendant greeted them. He led Emerald inside the building and took the elevator to the penthouse floor.

Frank took her coat and purse and hung them in the foyer closet, then led Emerald to the den and turned on some music. He poured two drinks, handing Emerald one of them.

"Relax, Emerald, make yourself at home," Frank said walking over to the window overlooking the city's beauty.

Emerald began to dance her way toward the music. She felt relaxed and didn't want the night to end. However, it was getting late, so she needed to get to business.

Frank started dancing close behind Emerald. She turned to face him, and he slid his arms around her waist. Going in for another kiss, Emerald stopped him, yet again.

"What's the problem, my precious gem?" Frank asked with base in his voice.

"Let me get a little more comfortable," Emerald said.

She unbuttoned her blouse and dropped her skirt to the floor. She kept her stiletto boots on for a wow effect. Frank could feel himself getting hard. Emerald smiled and coaxed him to come closer. He again grabbed her by the waist, but was more aggressive this time. The liquor kicked in, and he was good and ready. Frank led her down the hall to his bedroom and immediately started undressing.

He pulled Emerald into his embrace and kissed her neck, working his way up to her lips. This time she met his lips with hers and asked, "Are you paying with cash or credit?"

Frank opened his eyes with his lips still puckered and said, "wha...what?"

"Are you paying with cash or credit?" Emerald repeated.

Frank sat on the bed, placing his head in the palms of his hands. He couldn't believe what he was hearing.

"I'm sorry. Is there a problem?" Emerald questioned as she connected the square device to her phone.

"No problem. I mean, yes, it's a problem. I had no idea. You, you were a—" Emerald cut him off.

"Watch your words. I'm not anything. I just believe you should know better. You must pay to play," Emerald sarcastically said.

Emerald disconnected the square device from her phone. Her eyes met his, overwhelmed with pity. "You're too old not to know the game. You have to pay to play," she said.

Frank looked at Emerald, pointed to the door, and hollered, "Get the fuck out."

"What about my money for my time?" Emerald questioned.

Frank began walking towards her, but thought twice about getting physical with her. He grabbed his pants off the floor, pulled his wallet out, and started counting two one-hundred-dollar bills.

"It's five hundred," Emerald sternly said.

Frank stopped counting and took a deep breath. He continued counting five, one-hundred-dollar bills. Mumbling, this is the highest price I ever paid to dance and drink with a woman.

"I gave you a discount because you know Vera," Emerald said as she looked herself over in the mirror. Seeming satisfied with what she saw, she took the money from Frank's hand and kissed him on the cheek.

Walking back into the living room, Emerald quickly got dressed. As she placed the money in her purse, she looked around Frank's home and smiled. Calling out to Frank, "We could have had so much fun."

"Unbelievable," Frank cried.

"No ticky, no tocky," Emerald said as she closed the door behind her.

Heifer, you'll get enough of pulling up on these men and not telling them what's up initially. I don't want anybody taking me and having their way with me because you broke protocol.
~VB

Crime Scene

"Man, listen, I had this bad bitch over the other night. I could tell when I met her that she wasn't from around here. You know, she had her shit together." Manny boasted to his boys, Shane and Caleb.

"Every bitch you get with, you claim is badder than the last one," Shane said while passing the blunt to Caleb.

"Why, every time y'all talk about our sisters, they gotta be "bad bitches, or bitches"?" Caleb questioned after taking a pull off the blunt, Shane passed him.

Manny and Shane looked at each other, then at Caleb. "Man, don't start with that Nubian Queen shit," they said at once.

"Whatever!" Caleb said taking a long pull off the blunt and put it out.

"Can I finish my story, Captain-Save-A-Hoe?" Manny said as he stared at Caleb and chuckled.

Caleb nodded as he sat back on the sofa and patiently listened to Manny finish his story.

"As I was sayin', the bitch was bad. Good job, her own crib, no kids, and no nigga. She claims her last relationship was a year ago," Manny said wiping his face as if drying off after a swim.

"A year ago? Get the fuck out of here. You know how bitches be lying," Shane said shaking his head in disbelief.

"I swear to God, that's what she said. As long as I get the pussy, I'm not tryin' to do any background checks. You feel me," Manny said defensively.

The room was uncomfortably quiet for a moment. The football game played in the background as Manny reached for a beer bottle.

"Can I please finish my story uninterrupted?" Manny said as he took a drink from his beer bottle. Both Shane and Caleb motioned with a head nod for Manny to continue.

"Shit got heated quickly. She's all over me like a dog on a bone. I'm thinkin', damn, this chic feelin' a brutha. That new joint by Cardi and Meg comes on, and obviously, it must be her song because she jumps up and starts twerkin' all in my face. I did everything I could not to bust at that moment."

"Thirsty ass!" Caleb mumbles, causing Shane to chuckle. Manny was so caught up in his story that he kept talking, not realizing what was said.

"She starts strippin' for a brutha, then takes my clothes off. Now I'm feelin' like a bitch. But the way that ass was jigglin' like jingle bell, I didn't say a word. I held my joint, waiting for her to bounce on it. She pulls out her phone and starts recordin'. I'm hidin' my face because y'all know what's up."

"No face, no case!" the three of them shout as they dap it up.

Manny pulls out his phone, searches through his video album, and hands the phone to Shane and Caleb.

Shane and Caleb stopped joking and became more interested in the story as they watched the video—both gray joggers, at attention.

"She got a friend or two?" Shane asked, damn near drooling.

"Typical sister, not knowing her worth," Caleb said as he pushed the phone toward Manny.

"Fuck outta here!" Manny and Shane said to Caleb.

"I couldn't take it anymore; I grabbed her by the waist and bent her over the couch. I commence to wearin' that ass out; I'm talking balls deep in her guts. She was giving it back to me, too, pound for pound. Juices are all over me. I'm thinkin', it has been a year since she's been with anybody," Manny says as his excitement to finish telling the story dwindles.

"And then what? Man, don't leave us hangin'!" Shane eagerly says.

"She pushes me away and says, 'give her a minute,' then grabs her clothes and runs to the bathroom. Maybe she's havin' "fucker's remorse" or some shit. I don't know. So, I go behind her and knock on the door—no answer. I start

16

bangin' on the door, but still no answer. I twist the knob, and the door opens a little. She slams the door in my face and tries to lock it, but not before I can get it open again. I ask her: 'What's up? What's the problem?' She starts cryin' and apologizin'."

"Don't tell me she cried rape?" Shane asked, surprised.

"Man, hell no!" Manny growled.

Shane pretended to be ill. "I feel sick, Manny. Don't tell me that chick is a dude?"

"Nigga you got one more time, and I'm going to throw your ass out on your neck," Manny said through gritted teeth.

"What, then?" Caleb asked.

"She started her period, bitch had blood all over me, my couch, my chair," Manny said in a fake tearful voice.

Shane jumped up from the chair he was sitting in and wiped down the back of his sweatpants. Caleb laughed as Manny mean-mugged him.

"It was like a crime scene when I finally got in the bathroom. Blood was dripping down her legs. She stood before the sink cleaning herself up with my white towels," Manny said in a low voice, staring off as if reliving the scene again.

Shane nor Caleb could contain their laughter. Manny dropped his head in defeat as they shouted, "Death to a bad bitch with good pussy!"

Girl, how old are we? You should know by now when I'm going to be sick. Out here embarrassing me. Get yourself together. Holla at me in seven days.
~VB

Jump Start

"This is what I'll do to get you in the mood," Rome sang in his best Scottie from The Whisper's voice while busying himself around his condo.

He had an old soul to be in his prime at 37 years of age. Rome had just finished preparing dinner, uncorking the champagne, and was hopeful for a romantic encounter with Hazel. She was the Hiring Manager of his marketing firm. Hazel, being more seasoned, made Rome a bit nervous. She was 25 years his senior, but she looked every bit of maybe 40ish, with a banging body, cute in the face, tiny waist, and an ass that screamed collard greens and cornbread. The chemistry brewing between them was electrifying. He finally mustered up the nerve to ask her to accompany him for a home-cooked meal at his place. Hazel was all too eager to oblige Rome's request.

Ding Dong! Rome heard the bell chime. Looking at his security monitor, he could see Hazel at the door. He looked around his condo, ensuring everything was in place, before buzzing her in.

Rome opened the door just as Hazel made it to the top step. He greeted her, "Hello, beautiful!"

"Hello yourself, handsome!" Hazel cooed as she stepped inside.

Rome embraced Hazel before taking her coat and hanging it in the hall closet.

Hazel thanked him as she admired the art on the walls. *He's truly a man, matured past his years*, she thought.

"It smells delicious in here!" Hazel said as she followed Rome to the kitchen.

"Thank you, I cooked my famous lasagna, salad, and garlic bread," Rome proudly stated.

"Famous?" Hazel questioned with a raised brow.

"My family approved it," Rome said with hesitation.

Hazel sat at the table and watched Rome move around the kitchen with ease. She loved a man that could cook.

Rome poured two glasses of champagne, offering Hazel one of them.

Hazel took the glass with a smile. "What are we celebrating?" she asked.

"You...us?" Rome smoothly stated.

"Oh," Hazel stated as she raised her glass to his and took a sip. Her nose wiggled at the tickling of the champagne bubbles.

Rome fixed two plates and placed one on the table in front of Hazel and the other in front of the chair to her right.

He sat down, grabbed her hand, and said grace. When he looked up, Hazel was looking at him with astonishment.

"Did I do something wrong?" Rome asked.

"No, sir. Everything about you is right," Hazel said before tasting her first fork full of lasagna. Closing her eyes, she savored the taste, silently thanking God for the delicious meal and Rome.

They continued eating, with small talk and lots of champagne.

Hazel was very relaxed at this point. Rome asked if she wanted something a bit stronger. Hazel requested whiskey. "My girl!" Rome mumbled as he led her to the sofa.

He strolled over to the bar, poured two whiskeys neat, then went and sat on the sofa next to Hazel and handed her a glass.

She raised her glass towards Rome. "To a new relationship."

"Cheers," Rome seductively stated.

Rome turned up the music that had been playing softly in the background. He gently pulled Hazel by the hand, guiding her to stand up. Placing his arms around her waist and pulling her close to him, they swayed back and forth to the beat of the music.

Hazel was in heaven; Rome was giving her all the feels tonight. Feelings she didn't know she needed. After her husband of forty years passed away two years ago, she hadn't dated anyone. It was nice to feel a man's touch.

Rome spun Hazel around, not missing a beat of the music. He softly sang along to Luther Vandross and Cheryl Lynn's, If This World Was Mine. They both thought, *what a perfect night.*

Hazel was feeling herself as she said, "Alexa, play Pussycat by Missy Elliott."

Rome appeared shocked and turned on at the same time. Hazel pushed him onto the couch and began to dance seductively in front of him. Rome was thoroughly enjoying the show.

Hazel began to sing as she wound her hips and dropped her body low, almost to the floor, then slowly brought herself back up, causing Rome to grab her waist and pull her onto his lap.

Rome unzipped the back of Hazel's dress. They slowly undressed one another, kissing and touching various parts of the other's body along the way.

Hazel continued to sing, "pussy don't fail me now," with an uneasy chuckle.

Taking Hazel by the hand, Rome led her into his bedroom, laying her down softly on his bed. Hazel seemed a bit nervous. Rome lay on top of her as he looked into her eyes. He slowly tried to enter Hazel, but struggled to complete the task.

Hazel appeared to be in agony. Rome thought, *I know she's not a virgin at this age. Besides, she was married before I was born. Maybe it's due to her not having sex for two years.*

"Just relax," he whispered, while attempting to shove himself into her again.

Hazel's body began to tense as she gazed at Rome. "You young men don't know the first thing about making love. Everything is a race for you all."

"I can slow it down, baby. I'm sorry," Rome whispered. He was ready and didn't know how much longer he could wait.

"You must take your time with me. Give me extra attention. I'm like a vintage 69 Chevelle; you must ensure all my parts are oiled. Put the cables on me, Daddy." Hazel cooed.

"Like a jumpstart?" Rome questioned.

"You learn fast," Hazel said as she made a roaring sound.

Hazel girl, you are crazy! Why did you say to that man, 'put the cables on you'? I hope this young man isn't afraid for the rest of his life after being with an older woman. However, thank you for protecting me. You know how painful sex can be once you go through menopause.
~VB

I Deserve

I deserve a life of love, unconditional love. I deserve healthy relationships. I deserve multiple orgasms. I deserve to say no, not to be ridiculed or taken advantage of. I deserve to be healthy and cared for. I have a right to wear my hair, long, short, or bald.

Once a year to once every five years, I have an intimate date with my doctor. They get into my business and offer their opinion. I listen, and I follow all directions. I exercise and tighten, then release, especially after these kids ripped me a new one. I change my soaps, no perfumes, and wear cotton panties, at least in the middle—no douching, no multiple partners, latex condoms, water-based lube, blah blah blah.

After all this, I deserve to live and express myself however and whenever I choose to.

I DESERVE.

~VB

Quantity Over Quality

"Commitment is a fool's goal," Taye said as he got dressed.

Tracey looked on with disappointment while standing in her bedroom doorway. It had been two years since she met Taye, and she was still unsure of what her "title" was with him.

"I guess that makes me a fool, Taye. Not only have you not committed to marriage, but you won't even commit to being my boyfriend!" Tracey said in a wavered voice.

"You said it, not me," Taye said as he stopped and looked at Tracey with pity. He did love her, just not enough to give up Stacy, Kim, and Rhonda.

Tracey started feeling sick to her stomach. She didn't need Taye's pity and decided to keep it to herself. For the last four weeks, Tracey hadn't been feeling well. She had an upcoming appointment with her doctor in a few days.

"I can't keep doing this with you, Taye. Whatever this is makes me feel some type of way. I deserve better, and I thought you would give me that. Guess I was wrong about you," Tracey said as she fought back tears.

"Don't put that weight on me, Tracey. It's unfair to me that you want me to validate you. If you don't think highly of yourself, sweetheart, I can't make you do it. You have mostly women in your family. Didn't they teach you any girl power?" Taye sarcastically said. He began walking towards the door before Tracey had a chance to respond.

"So that's it? You're just going to leave in the middle of our conversation?" Tracey cried out.

"Listen, Tracey. I think we should just call it. You know, be done with this. I'm just not the man for you. You're a sweet woman; however, you're asking for a fairytale relationship. A relationship that I'm not ready to again, commit to." Taye sighed, kissed Tracey, and walked out the door.

"Fuck you too, Taye!" Tracey screamed. She was livid at Taye's response. She was even more livid at herself for wasting her time.

A few days later, Tracey could barely get out of bed. She was feeling stressed from the previous day's argument with Taye. Her body was sore, and she had the sniffles. Tracey began scrolling Instagram, searching Taye's page, hoping to find any answers to where their relationship went wrong. A woman commented on Taye's last three posts: *"Beware of this loser; he's not right. I haven't felt like myself since I started messing around with him."*

I feel you, Sis! Tracey thought.

Just as she started reading another comment, her phone rang. Her doctor's office informed her of a sooner appointment that was available that day. Tracey agreed and got up to shower and dress. She felt feverish as she did so.

Tracey entered the doctor's office and checked in at the front desk. Fifteen minutes later, a nurse called her name. She followed the nurse to room 3.

The nurse took Tracey's weight and motioned for her to sit. Upon taking her vitals, the nurse informed Tracey that her blood pressure was also high and she was running a fever of 102°F.

The nurse gave Tracey a cup to provide a urine sample.

"I'm not pregnant," Tracey quickly said.

"It's protocol," the nurse said with a smile.

Tracey strolled to the bathroom, trying to remember her last period: when it came, how long it stayed, and if there was anything out of the ordinary about it. She began praying that she wasn't pregnant. Taye wasn't father material. Hell, he wasn't any kind of material at this point.

Tracey handed the nurse her urine sample and sat back on the table. The nurse informed her the doctor would be in shortly.

After fifteen minutes, the doctor entered the room.

"Hello, Ms. Thornton. What brings you in today?" the doctor asked.

Tracey recounted her symptoms. "Well, the last few days, maybe a week, I've felt sick with a runny nose, my body sore, feverish, and fatigued."

"I see your vitals are slightly high. Have you been around anyone with covid symptoms?" the doctor asked as she typed on her laptop.

"No, not that I know of," Tracey said as she thought about her interactions over the last few weeks.

The doctor rechecked Tracey's vitals, breathing, etc. "Everything sounds good with your lungs. Your pregnancy test was negative. Your vitals are still high. It looks like it may be a virus. I've had numerous patients come in this month with similar symptoms," the doctor said as she continued to type on her laptop.

"Okay, that's a relief," Tracey said.

"I see it's time for your annual Pap smear and blood work. Would you like to take care of that while you're here?" the doctor asked. She stopped typing and looked up at Tracey.

"Sure, that would be fine," Tracey said.

The doctor handed Tracey a gown and stepped out of the room. Ten minutes later, she returned with a nurse. She motioned for Tracey to lay back and place her feet into each stirrup.

As protocol, she gave Tracey a heads-up about the procedure. The doctor informed Tracey to take a deep breath and exhale as the speculum was inserted. She expressed to Tracey that she would feel pressure and discomfort as she checked her cervix, took cultures, and asked if Tracey wanted to test for STIs and HIV. Tracey agreed as she adjusted her hips a bit due to the discomfort of the exam. The doctor apologized and moved as quickly as she could.

Once the exam was complete, the nurse sat Tracey up and prepped her arm for blood work.

The doctor told Tracey she would call her with the results in a couple of days.

Two days later, Tracey was feeling worse than the previous days. She didn't want to return to the doctor because it was just a virus. Knowing these things could sometimes take 7-14 days to run its course. She rested when she could. Working from home made it easy to do so.

Getting up to make lunch, she decided to scroll Instagram. The first post she saw was Taye at the gym. *Damn, this man is so fine,* Tracey thought. Another pic of him didn't do him any justice. *Perhaps he was having a bad day,* she thought.

Tracey went straight to Taye's page and looked at all his posts since their last encounter. She noticed Taye's appearance had drastically changed, so she decided to send Taye a text message:

Tracey: Hey Taye, just checking on you.

Taye: I'm good; wtf is everybody so worried about me?

Tracey: I can't speak for everyone else. I guess I caught you on a bad day.

Take care!

Taye: I should have taken care before I ever messed with any of you bitches!

Tracey: Wow! Really Taye? That's what we're doing now, name-calling?

While Tracey waited for Taye's response, she had an incoming call from her doctor.

"Hello, this is Tracey," she said as she placed the phone on speaker.

"Hello, Ms. Thornton. This is Dr. Panna. I wanted to know if you could come into the office for your results?"

"And why can't you just tell me over the phone like you normally do?" Tracey nervously asked.

"Well, some of the results are a bit sensitive. Will you be able to come to the office today?" the doctor asked.

"I'm on my way now," Tracey said. She quickly slid her feet into her Crocs, grabbed her purse, keys, and rushed out the door.

"Great, see you soon," the doctor said.

Tracey was very nervous as she drove to the doctor's office. It was only five miles away, but it seemed like a road trip. Her thoughts were going a mile a minute. *What the hell could be wrong that she couldn't tell me over the phone?*

She stopped in her tracks when she walked into the doctor's office. Of all people, Taye was sitting in the waiting area.

"Why are you here?" he asked.

"Why else do people come to the doctor, Taye?" Tracey sarcastically said.

"Don't get smart, Ms. Thornton," Taye said through gritted teeth.

"Ms. Thornton," the nurse called.

Tracey hesitated before walking through the door. The nurse again took her to room three.

"The doctor will be in shortly," she said.

Another nurse called Taye's name, "Mr. Banks."

Taye jumped up and walked through the same doors Tracey went through. The same nurse took him to room two.

The doctor entered the room designated for Tracey to share with her the results. With a stern look, she said, "Ms. Thornton, I'm sorry to inform you that your HIV test results are positive."

"Okay, and what does that mean?" Tracey asked without thinking. The doctor's words had not registered in Tracey's brain.

The doctor let out a heavy sigh. "Tracey, I understand that this is a lot to take in, but what this means is that... your immune system has been compromised. Is there someone I can call for you?" the doctor gently responded.

Out of nowhere, Tracey began feeling warm, her palms grew sweaty, her heart sank, and her ears started ringing loudly.

"Omg, Ms. Thornton, are you alright?" Tracey could vaguely hear someone saying.

Tracey began coming to. She didn't understand how she wound up on the floor. Her head was pounding. Regaining conscious of her surroundings made her realize the ringing in her ears was coming from her voice screaming. "I'm going to kill that bastard in room two!"

"I'm sorry, Ms. Thornton. What about room two?" the doctor asked.

"That motherfucker in room two, Mr. Taye Banks, gave me HIV! He fucks every woman he encounters! He doesn't care about anyone but himself! I know it was that nasty bastard, and I want him locked under the jail for what he's done to me!" Tracey cried.

"Ms. Thornton, please calm down," the doctor pleaded.

"Calm down? How! And you just gave me a death sentence?" Tracey screamed.

Tracey sat in the chair closest to the door and began to take deep breaths. She began to pray, then cry. The doctor motioned for the nurse to hand her a box of tissues. She took a few and gave them to Tracey.

"Ms. Thornton, please, is there anyone we can call for you?" the nurse pleaded.

Tracey thought for a moment. "Yes, call my brother T. 555-1212."

The nurse dialed the number as directed, while the doctor stood rubbing Tracey's back.

As the nurse began to speak, Tracey snatched the phone. "Taye, you low down, dirty, good for nothing, nasty, selfish narcissist. How could you? Do you just hook up with random women? We were in a relationship for two years, and you knew what you were doing with them. Then you come and have unprotected sex with me. You would rather pick quantity over quality?"

Taye hung up the phone, walked out of his exam room, and into room three.

"Excuse you, sir," The doctor and nurse said in unison.

"No, let him in!" Tracey said in a wavered voice as tears streamed down her face.

"You are a nagging, selfish, all-I-want-is-love-and-a-husband, fuck it-I'll-take-a-boyfriend-ass- bitch. How dare you blame me. Just as you verbalized my resume of sexual partners and how I knew what I was doing and still came to your bed, you play a part in this, too. You invited me into your bed, knowing I had many women. Or, as you say, I chose quantity over quality. If you allowed me to have unprotected sex with you, knowing all this, what quality of a woman are you? All of you knew what kind of man I was, and all of you decided to get whatever piece of me you could. To do what? That's right, satisfy your needs! Therefore, I will never commit to anything except me. I'm number one bitch, and don't you forget it! As far as suing me, for perhaps, knowingly giving you HIV, get in line bitch, and take a chair because it's around the corner!"

Yes, we can blame heartbreak on those we trust our hearts to. However, you are responsible for you. Take responsibility for the part you play in your demise.
~VB

Sin'n and Grin'n

"I haven't heard from you in two weeks," Guy said through the phone while pacing back and forth in the living room. He and Valerie had been talking, or more like arguing, over the phone for the past 20 minutes.

"Don't start, Guy! I've been very busy with work. Damn, give me a chance to miss you. We don't have to talk every day," Valerie said with irritation as she walked into her office. She muted the phone and greeted her staff.

"VALERIE!" Guy angrily shouted.

"Later, Guy!" Valerie calmly said before ending the call. She had no time or patience for anyone who treated her less than she deserved.

Guy looked at his phone and saw the call had ended. Furious that she hung up on him, he dialed her number and got her voicemail. "That's it! If this is how she wants to play it, so be it. I'm over it!" he shouted to himself.

Grabbing his backpack, shades, and helmet, he stormed out of the house and hopped on his motorcycle. He approached the stop sign two blocks from his home and did a stop-and-roll before turning. Out of nowhere, an SUV hit his back wheel, causing his motorcycle to hit the curb. Guy flipped over the handlebars and onto his back. He felt a sharp pain move down his spine. He lay there struggling to breathe from the throbbing pain in his back.

The driver of the SUV kept going. A bystander rushed to Guy's side and asked if he was alright. Guy sat up and took his helmet off. The bystander stated she was a nurse and could help him. Guy waved her off and noted the only thing wrong with him was a bruised ego. Then, he stood up and examined his motorcycle, feeling relieved there was no significant damage.

"By the way, I'm Lisa," the bystander stated.

"Nice to meet you, Nurse Lisa," Guy said, smiling as he held out his hand.

Lisa shook his hand and looked at him with a raised brow.

"Sorry, I'm Guy," he said as he mounted his motorcycle.

"Are you sure you're okay?" Lisa asked before stepping back and allowing Guy the room to back his motorcycle onto the street.

"I assure you, I'm fine," Guy said. He started his motorcycle.

"At least allow me to put my number in your phone. Just in case you start feeling any aches and pains later," Lisa said, holding out her hand.

"If I feel any aches or pains, perhaps I should see a doctor and not a nurse," Guy said, handing Lisa his phone.

They both chuckled as Lisa took the phone and added her name and number to Guy's contacts.

"'Nurse Lisa,'" Guy read the contact info aloud.

Lisa smiled and walked towards her car. Before getting in, she turned towards Guy, "Call me, regardless of how you feel."

"Bet," Guy said. He put his helmet on and rode off on his motorcycle.

Guy felt shaky from the fall as he pulled into his office parking lot. Walking into his office building, he went straight to his corner office and closed the door behind him. Taking out his phone, he scrolls to Valerie's name to text.

Guy: Call me when you can.

Valerie: I AM BUSY!!!

Guy: When you're not busy. Valerie, please, I was in an accident.

Valerie: Fine! Call me.

Guy immediately dialed Valerie's number. Again, the call went to voicemail.

He violently redialed the number. This time it went through.

"What?" Valerie answered nonchalantly.

"What?! Valerie, I was in an accident. A car hit me and knocked me off my motorcycle," Guy hesitantly said.

"Okay, did you die??? I guess not, since you're harassing me after I told you I was busy," Valerie said with a sigh.

"Wow, Valerie." Guy pleaded with questions. After three years, can you at least act concerned? What's going on with you? Did something happen that I'm unaware of?"

"It's nothing. I'm fine. You're fine. We're fine. Can I please get back to work?" Valerie responded sarcastically.

Before Guy could respond, Valerie ended the call. Guy slumped down in his chair, turning to face his laptop. He figured he would start his workday and forget about Valerie for the moment. Guy was still shaken from the accident and didn't want to stress himself out further.

The day went by quickly. After a couple of meetings, two pain pills for an excruciating headache, and two cups of coffee later, it was 5:00 pm. Guy closed his laptop and informed his team he was leaving for the day. Walking out of his office building, he noticed his motorcycle connected to a tow truck, and a police officer standing beside it.

"What is the meaning of this?" Guy asked as he looked back and forth between the tow truck driver and the officer.

"I'm just doing my job," the tow truck driver responded.

"This motorcycle was reported in an accident on 1st Ave and Home Street," the officer said, tearing a ticket from his book and handing it to Guy.

"You must be kidding me. Somebody hit me and kept going this morning!" Guy shouted.

"Calm down, buddy. Did you report the accident?" the officer asked as he placed his hand on his gun, holstered on his side.

"No. The driver kept going, and I just left since I wasn't hurt bad," Guy mumbled.

Between the arguing with Valerie before work, the accident, and the nurse, he realized reporting the accident hadn't crossed his mind. The officer signaled for the tow truck driver to leave.

As the officer walked towards his patrol car, he looked back at Guy and shook his head. Guy was fuming with anger. In that moment, he felt defeated in his relationship and the entire day. Taking his phone out of his jacket pocket, he dialed Valerie's number. Again, the call went straight to voicemail. He texted her and saw that her phone was on Do Not Disturb.

"Fuuuccckkk!" he screamed.

As he walked towards his office building, his phone buzzed. He answered without looking at the number. "Valerie, can you come get me? The police are here, and my motorcycle has been towed."

"Bruh, this ain't Valerie, but I'm calling about her. That accident was a warning. Stop all forms of communication with Valerie. She's finished with you," the unfamiliar voice said.

"Who is this? How can I not come near Valerie, and we live together? Did Valerie put you up to this? I'm having a fucked-up day, and I don't have time for games," Guy said through gritted teeth.

"Nah, Bruh. Valerie is sick of your shit. We moved her things out while you were at work," the caller said, laughing.

"What the hell is going on? Let me call Valerie," Guy said, ending the call.

Just as he dialed Valerie's number, a car pulled up to him with such speed it made him stumble and fall to the ground. A woman jumped out of the vehicle, with Valerie and Lisa following behind her. Valerie and Lisa laughed as Guy struggled to get off the ground.

"Valerie, why are you doing this to me? Nurse Lisa?" Guy said, confused.

"Valerie? Nurse Lisa?" Valerie said, mocking Guy.

"You don't remember me?" Lisa questioned as she walked up to Guy.

"Remember you from this morning? Of course, I do," Guy said as he stepped back, watching all three of them.

"This morning, huh? So, you're acting like you weren't sin'n and grin'n with me for six months last year?" Lisa said, staring at Guy in disbelief.

Guy got a good look at Lisa and began to stutter, "I um, wow, Jalisa? You look different. Wait, how do you know Valerie?"

"Impossible, she looks that different if you were with her for six months!" Valerie shouted, charging towards Guy.

"Friend, slow down. We came here for you to tell this clown to get the fuck on," the woman said as she held Valerie back.

"Friend?!" Guy questioned.

The woman, Valerie, and Lisa all shouted, "Yes, friend!"

"You don't deserve us," the woman tearfully said.

"Who the fuck are you, dude?" Guy questioned.

The woman took off her shades and hat. "Do you know me now?" she questioned.

Guy looked as if he had seen a ghost. "Monae?"

"Yes, Monae! It was easy for you to forget about me and our son. You chased after me two years ago, showering me with anything I wanted until I gave in. You got me pregnant, waited for the baby to be born, and forced me to put our son through a DNA test. Once you found out you were the father, you ghosted us."

"Mr. Guy "Sin'n and Grin'n" Benjamin. You're out here living triple lives and have the nerve to look confused and appalled. It's over!" Valerie shouted.

"Bravo. You bitches think y'all got me? Huh? Y'all ain't got shit. So what I had all three of you, I never lied to any of you. I never promised a commitment other than living with Valerie. Oops, she lived with me because she had nowhere to go. That's why she pretended to be blind to my extracurricular activities. Didn't you, Valerie?" Guy said, pointing back and forth between the women.

"Don't answer him," Lisa tearfully said, while consoling Valerie.

"Don't cry now. You heauxs weren't crying when y'all ran up on me. Did any of you cry when y'all put this weak-ass plan together? What did y'all think I would do, feel sorry and apologize. Fuck outta here," Guy laughed as he began walking towards his office building.

"Guy!" all three women shouted.

Guy turned around, shocked, to see all three women with guns pointed at him. Just as he was about to speak, on the count of three, the women fired their weapons, riddling his body with bullets. Guy fell to the ground, his body shaking violently. Loud, excruciating screams filled the parking lot. Guy clawed at the ground as he choked on his own blood.

Once the shooting stopped, he attempted to open his eyes. All he could see was a white light and the feeling of heat on his face. His body shook once more, and he could hear his name. His eyes flew open, and he quickly sat up.

"Guy, are you okay?" his wife Keisha asked.

"Mama is daddy, okay?" His three daughters, Valerie, Lisa, and Monae, asked.

"I'm fine, I'm fine," Guy said with a look of confusion on his face.

"Daddy had a nightmare on Elm Street," Valerie said as she laughed. Her sisters joined in the laughter as they all left out of the den where Guy had been napping.

Keisha suspiciously looked at Guy and said, you reap what you sow. You've messed over women your entire life, and now you're dreaming of the same thing happening to your daughters. Ironically, you're their perpetrator.

Guy wiped the sweat from his brow and silently cried.

Don't cry. Just get your shit together!

~ VB

Time After Time

I've worn many hats, called by many titles. I was great at every one of them, and just the same, I failed at least once at all of them.

I've loved many people, but the ones I gave my heart to the most, unfortunately, did the most damage to my heart. Go figure.

Good and bad friends have come and gone, but my best friend was me.

Family, what can I say? You can't live with them, and you can't live without them...NOT!

Friend, family, or foe, you will be removed like weeds if you don't add to my growth.

I mean this from the bottom of my heart and soul.
~VB

Razzle Dazzle

"Just promise me you'll come home for dinner tonight," Tammy pleaded after Frank as he prepared for work.

Frank playfully mocked Tammy. "Just promise me you'll come home for dinner tonight."

Tammy shot Frank a dirty look. Frank chuckled, saying, "You Toussaint women are so demanding."

"I'll show you demanding," Tammy warned, waving the spoon, she was stirring the pot with as if she would pop Frank with it.

Frank backed away in defeat, knowing Tammy would swing if she were close enough. He said his goodbyes and dashed out the back door.

Tammy noticed that Frank did not take his work bag or give her a goodbye kiss. Focusing back on dinner, she began singing, "A sprinkle of this for love, a pinch of that for grounding, a dash of this for commitment, perhaps two for reassurance, and the mind goes forever here, and the eyes go somewhere out there, for my love."

She smiled as she remembered her grandmother teaching her that song many moons ago.

The day went by hastily. Tammy was so busy with dinner, housework, and facilitating a women's healing class, that she hadn't noticed Frank was an hour late for dinner. Nor had he called to state he would be home late. Tammy became furious as she reached for her phone to call Frank.

After several rings, his phone went to voicemail. She closed her eyes and took a deep breath to ground herself. Then, she opened her eyes and grabbed her purse, car keys, and the plate she prepared for Frank.

Traffic was mild as she raced in and out of the I-90 lanes. She began repeatedly singing the lyrics to the song her grandmother taught her: "A sprinkle of this for love, a pinch of that for grounding, a dash of this for commitment, perhaps two for reassurance, and the mind goes forever here, and the eyes go somewhere out there, for my love."

When she reached her destination, she pulled into a driveway, exited her car, and gracefully walked up the porch stairs to the front door. The door was slightly open. She heard the sound of a well-known melody floating softly through the air, and a familiar voice beckoning her to enter.

Tammy looked around before entering the home, then pushed the door open and entered. The song began again. As she approached, she noticed Frank sitting in the middle of a circle of women tied to a chair. His head slumped to the right, with his chin touching his chest. As the singing became louder, Frank looked towards Tammy, almost as if he was looking through her. His eyes looked void.

Tammy looked at each woman with mixed emotions, full of fear, admonishment, and excitement. "Thanks, ladies. Please take a seat."

She spoke with boldness and love. "As you all know, we are gathered here for the sacrament of yet another fallen husband. Some of you said mine was no different, and I begged to differ. With sadness, I will be the first to admit I was wrong. Frank, Frank, Frank! I gave you full instructions this morning, and of course, you didn't follow them."

Frank began to moan as he tried to wiggle his hands-free. "It's no use." The women sang in unison.

"That's right, Frank, it's no use," Tammy said. As she uncovered the plate of food, she brought for Frank. One of the ladies passed Tammy a fork.

Tammy took a deep breath and forced Frank to eat the entire plate as the ladies began to sing: "A sprinkle of this for love, a pinch of that for grounding, a dash of this for commitment, perhaps two for reassurance, and the mind goes forever here, and the eyes go somewhere out there, for my love."

As the ladies kept singing, a man for every woman came out of the shadows and sat next to Frank. Coaching him to submit to his wife: "Don't fight it, brother, she knows what's best for you. You'll love it here; we all do!"

The women began to smile as Tammy nodded her head in approval.

Frank's neck stiffened as his eyes lit up. A smile crept on his face as he looked at Tammy.

"Yes, Frank, you'll love it here," she said before smashing the plate across Frank's head.

As blood trickled down the right side of Frank's face, Tammy took the hemline of her skirt and wiped it away.

The women began to smile as they shouted, "Completion!" Tammy nodded her head in approval.

The men looked at Frank and shouted, "The bro code is no longer!" All the women clapped their hands in approval.

Tammy began to speak, "I'm so proud of you ladies for completing your last class today. It's a shame I had to sacrifice my own for the greater good of womanhood. But as the saying goes: 'every dog has its day.' Too bad, this time, the dog was mine."

The women empathized with Tammy, saying, "We've all been there."

Tammy gave a half smile as she looked around the room.

"Where is the woman Frank was creeping with?" Tammy asked.

A young woman stepped forward with fear in her eyes. She was pleading through body language, too afraid to speak.

The room grew quiet while Tammy examined the woman as if she were prey. The woman started shivering. Tammy stepped so close to the woman air couldn't fit between them.

All the women began to step forward and repeatedly chant, "Whore!"

The chanting caused the woman to cower to the floor.

"You whore!" Tammy shouted. Her loudness caused the room to go silent.

"Whore?! Ha, if that's not the pot calling the kettle black! You're all no better than me. I may have slept with your husband, but you continued to sleep with him knowing what he was into. I guess we both were desperate for a piece of man. Your so-called sisterhood is no better. They all slept with him too!" the woman spat with laughter.

"That's a lie!" the sisterhood of women shouted.

Frank began laughing hysterically. The other husbands stared Frank down, knowing his M-O was a womanizer.

"Is this true, Frank?" Tammy questioned with desperation.

"Don't question me, woman," Frank said before going in and out of consciousness.

An animal-like sound came from Tammy as she cheered "Die!" repeatedly. She circled the room, tapping every woman's shoulder who stood before her. The women began crying as they dropped to the floor, while the men watched silently in horror.

When Tammy reached the last woman, she asked, "Why would you all try to play me? You knew my supernatural powers, yet you all came for me and tried to make a fool of me. Mistook my kindness for weakness."

Before the woman could answer, Tammy spat out, "Die," causing the last woman to drop to the floor. Then, she began walking towards the front door, remaining silent until she reached the front porch. Closing the door behind her, she whispered, "Burn."

The house immediately went up in flames, causing Frank to laugh hysterically again, saying, "I told y'all she was crazy." The men cried in anguish as Tammy drove away from the scene.

Tammy, why did you do those people like that? Over no good ass Frank?! Oh well, on to the next one.

~VB

For The Love of Money

I never wanted for anything as a kid. Now that I'm twenty-one and living alone, I'm not about to starve, Jazzie thought as she lay in bed, thinking of her next move. Suddenly her phone buzzed, breaking her train of thought. She rolled on her side and took the phone off the nightstand. Seeing the name on the screen made her take a deep breath before answering.

"How can I help you, Harlem?" Jazzie nonchalantly asked.

"My money you owe me," Harlem said through gritted teeth.

"I told you. You will get it when I get it," Jazzie said, rolling her eyes at the phone.

"I can think of a few ways you can pay me back if you can't come up with the money," Harlem said in a low tone.

Jazzie tensed at Harlem's suggestion.

"Hello?" Harlem responded as he looked at the phone, thinking Jazzie ended the call.

"I'm here, Harlem. The answer is no. I told you the last time; that was the last time," Jazzie said as she sucked her teeth. She hated Harlem. However, he did help her out when needed.

"Don't make me come over there and help you with your tone," Harlem spat.

Jazzy responded in a quiet tone. "I'm cool. It's cool. I have to go."

"I thought so. You have 48 hours to pay up, or I'll see you on the stage," Harlem growled before ending the call.

Jazzie rolled on her back and screamed, thinking, *WTF am I going to do! I can't call my parents because they think I'm working as a paid intern at a law firm. If they find out I dropped out of school, they are going to kill me. My aunt Jazlean (my namesake) talks too damn much, and she'll surely tell my mom.*

"Think, Jazzie, think!" Jazzie screamed.

Feeling defeated, Jazzie got out of bed and headed to the bathroom to shower. Following that, she casually threw on some cutoff denim shorts, a yellow tank, and white thong sandals. Reaching for the door, she quickly stopped in her tracks, remembering she had no gas. Jazzie pulled her phone out of her purse and dialed the only person she knew would help her at a hefty cost—Harlem.

"What Jazzie?" Harlem answered.

"I need a ride," Jazzie said in a low voice, barely audible.

"Come again, say what now?" Harlem questioned.

"I know this idiot heard me," Jazzie mumbled as she rolled her eyes at the phone.

"I need a ride, Harlem."

"That's what I thought you said. Please explain how that's any of my business," he said, nonchalantly.

"It's not your business, but since we're friends, I thought you would do me this favor," Jazzie pleaded.

"Step outside. My brother will take you where you need to go," Harlem ordered.

"How long?" Jazzie asked.

"NOW!" Harlem shouted.

Jazzie ran out the door without responding to Harlem. Harlem ended the call.

Jazzie was pissed that Harlem's brother, Reg, was readily available outside her apartment. She walked to the car with hesitation.

"Are you getting in, or what?" Reg asked with irritation.

"I don't know why Harlem mess with you birdbrains," he mumbled, licking his lips while looking at Jazzie's legs.

Jazzie got in the car and sat as close to the door as possible. She cringed at him, licking his chapped lips as he stared her up and down.

"You one of them stripper bitches?" Reg asked with excitement.

"The name is Jazzie. I ain't nobodies bitch, and I'm not a dancer," she said with disgust.

"The way that ass looks in those shorts, you need to be on that pole," Reg said as he pulled out into traffic.

Jazzie threw her hands up angrily. "Just drive, bro!"

"Where am I driving to, shorty? Reg questioned. My bad...Jazzie," he said, sarcastically.

Before Jazzie could answer, she noticed a black van pull up beside Reg's car. In the blink of an eye, the van sped up and cut in front of them, causing Reg to hit his brakes.

"Stupid motherfucker!" Reg shouted.

Jazzie looked from Reg to the van, wondering what was going on. She knew Harlem and his brother were always into something shady.

The passenger jumped out of the van and quickly approached the driver's side of the car.

Reg reached under the driver's seat for his gun. He was suddenly frantic. It wasn't there.

"Damn," Reg said.

"What's happening?" Jazzie frantically asked.

"Shut the fuck up and follow my lead," Reg said angrily.

The passenger busted the window with the butt of his gun, causing Reg and Jazzie to cower from the breaking glass. Then he aimed the gun at Reg's head.

"Get the fuck out of the car!" the passenger shouted.

Jazzie raised both hands in the air. "I don't have anything to do with this!" Jazzie cried.

"Bitch put your hands down," Reg said through gritted teeth.

"Both of y'all shut the fuck up and get out of the car," the passenger said angrily.

Reg slowly exited the car as his mind raced to find an escape.

Crying hysterically, Jazzie got out of the car and quickly walked around to the driver's side. The passenger grabbed her by the arm, pulling her to his side. He led them both to the van, forcing them into the back passenger door and quickly getting in, closing the door behind them. Wasting no time, the driver sped off into traffic in broad daylight.

"Do you know who the fuck I am?" Reg questioned.

"A dead motherfucker if you keep talking," said the passenger while aiming the gun at Reg's face.

"We don't have to do this, Yo. Let me make a phone call, and I can get you more money than you ever saw." Reg reached for his phone in his pocket.

The passenger put the gun to Reg's head, "Hands where I can see them nigga! Shorty, get the phone out of his pocket," he ordered.

"What's the number?" The passenger asked.

Reg hesitated before speaking up. "It's stored under Bro."

The passenger motioned for Jazzie to look through the phone and make the call. Jazzie placed the call and put the phone on speaker.

"Yo," Harlem said.

"Harlem, Harlem!" Jazzie cried out.

"Who the fuck? Jazzie? Why the fuck you got Reg's phone?" Harlem questioned.

"Yo, Bro. We got a problem," Reg said as calmly as possible. He couldn't show any fear.

"What problem? Where the fuck are you? Somebody better start talking now," Harlem growled in the phone.

Jazzie began to cry harder. Causing Harlem and Reg to shout in unison, "Shut the fuck up, bitch!"

"No, you shut the fuck up bitch!" Jazzie calmly said as she kicked Reg in the stomach. Causing him to double over in pain.

"I'm running this show," Jazzie said with a chuckle.

Reg looked up in shock. Harlem was quiet on the phone, trying to figure out what was happening.

"Don't get quiet now, Harlem. You usually got so much to say," Jazzie spat.

"I'm going to do damage to you when this is over, bitch!" Reg moaned in pain.

Jazzie looked at the passenger and nodded towards Reg.

The passenger eyed Reg and said, "Lights out nigga!"

Suddenly Reg felt a swift blow to the head with the butt of the gun. On the other end of the phone, Harlem could hear a loud thump and moaning as dazed Reg's head hit the dashboard.

"If y'all hurt my brother, this shit not gone end well!"

"Yeah, whatever. Two million dollars, and you'll see Reg unharmed in twenty-four hours," Jazzie said.

"Two million dollars? I don't have that kind of money," Harlem lied.

Jazzie nodded at the passenger once again. Without hesitation, he pulled the trigger and shot Reg in the knee. Reg belted a deep loud cry.

"Okay, goddammit, okay!" Harlem shouted. He was a fearless man, but family was his weakness.

"As I was saying, two million dollars and Reg lives. Meet me at the Bean in one hour. Come alone and no guns," Jazzie demanded as she ended the call. The Bean was on the top floor of a parking garage downtown. She directed the driver to head straight there. She needed her plan to work and didn't trust Harlem.

Her original plan was to have her guys follow her to the strip club and kidnap Harlem. However, she had no gas in her car and had to call him for a ride. Because she owed Harlem five thousand dollars, she knew he would have

Reg watching her every move, so switching her plan was easy.

Like clockwork, Harlem showed up. He got out of his car with a black leather duffel bag in hand.

Jazzy called him from Reg's phone, "Bring the bag to the black van parked to your right."

Harlem walked over to the van. The passenger swung the door open.

Casting a piercing gaze at Jazzie he asked, "Where's Reg?"

Before she could answer, Reg moaned, "I'm here."

Harlem stuck his head in the van and found Reg strapped in the seat tightly coiled in brown rope.

Jazzie snatched the bag of money and nodded at the passenger.

"Lights out," the passenger said. WHOP!

***

About an hour later, Harlem came to. The throbbing pain from the blow to the head forced him to slowly open his eyes to a pitch-black space. Startled and confused, he immediately yelled, "Reg! Reg! Reggie!"

Jazzie chuckled. "Your brother is right next to you."

Both men were tied back-to-back against a pole. The lights came on, and Harlem and Reg realized they were at their strip club. Jazzie nodded at the passenger, and music began blasting through the speakers, "'Bands a make her dance.'"

Worming her body seductively, she peeled off $5,000 from the bag of money Harlem gave her. Sprinkling the money around the brothers as she swayed her hips back and forth infuriated them. She gave them a naughty glance as she slowly began moving toward them on her hand and knees. In a sensual, yet mocking tone she said, "Is this what you like, Harlem, me dancing on stage and paying you the 5k I owe you?"

"You're a dead bitch!" Reg shouted.

Harlem followed. "So is your family!"

Jazzie slowly rolled her hips as she got up from the floor, refusing to take her eyes off of them. Then, exchanging with Harlem the same piercing stare, he casted earlier, she nodded. POW! The passenger shot Reg in the head. Before Harlem could make a sound, the driver sent a scorching slug through his heart.

"Brainless and heartless," Jazzie said as she made the holy trinity sign across her body, while snickering.

Turning towards the passenger with a sharp gaze, she added, "Let's settle up." Jazzie reached into the money-bag, grabbed the gun Harlem had tucked away, shot the passenger, and whispered, "Light's out."

Then she took the footage from the cameras, cut the music and lights, and locked the doors—swanning out into the humid Chicago streets without a care in the world.

For the love of money....Jazzie, you are colder than polar bear coochie!
~VB

Rebel

Rebel nervously waited, as she sat alone at the table, sipping on water. She asked La'Nard to meet her at The Weekend, a restaurant in Chicago's West Loop neighborhood.

"Hey beautiful. Sorry I'm running late, traffic on I-290 was terrible," La'Nard humbly expressed, as he sat before Rebel.

"No problem," Rebel said as she gazed from La'Nard to the waitress.

The waitress walked over to their table with pen and pad in hand, requesting La'Nard's drink of choice.

"I'll have a Gentleman Jack on the rocks."

"I'll have more water and lemon," said Rebel.

La'Nard looked at Rebel with a raised brow. "Water? You're going to allow me to drink alone," he asked.

"I'm not in the mood for alcohol, La'Nard," said Rebel in a low pitch, barely giving La'Nard any eye contact.

La'Nard was used to moody women all his life. Because of his mom and sisters, he knew to tread lightly at certain times with Rebel.

"No problem, love. Let's enjoy our evening of food and live music," said La'Nard with a smile.

Rebel returned the smile as she adjusted her chair to face toward the stage.

The waitress returned with their drinks. "Are you all ready to place your food order?" she pleasantly asked.

"I'll have the Caesar salad and jerk chicken pasta," Rebel said.

"And for you sir?" the waitress quickly asked. She knew Rebel had been waiting for some time, and therefore, wanted to get their order in.

"I'll have what the beautiful lady is having," La'Nard said, motioning towards Rebel.

As the waitress took their menu's and walked away, La'Nard held up his glass towards Rebel, "To us! May we fall in love over and over again." Rebel touched her glass to his and nodded.

"Okay Rebel. What's good? You seem off. I thought you asked me here for a date night, except it seems like you don't want to be here," La'Nard said, feeling uneasy.

Just as Rebel was about to speak, the emcee came on stage to announce the band. La'Nard continued to stare at Rebel, waiting for an answer. Rebel kept her attention towards the stage, with a look of relief. The waitress returned with their food order, as the band walked out on stage.

La'Nard took one glimpse at the drummer and downed his drink in a single gulp. "I know damn well you didn't call me here to see your father play tonight. You know he hates me."

"He doesn't hate you La'Nard. He just doesn't understand you," Rebel said, as she waved at her dad.

"Hate. Misunderstand. What's the difference Rebel?"

Rebel hunched her shoulders and began to clap as the band started to play. La'Nard ate his food and ordered another drink, choosing to table the conversation for the remainder of the band's set. He couldn't understand why Rebel was being so difficult tonight. This was out of character for her. It wasn't just mood swings, something was up—something she wasn't telling him.

After the band's first set, Rebel's dad, Benjamin, came over to greet them. "Hey Baby-girl, so glad you could make it," Benjamin said, as he kissed Rebel on the cheek.

He nodded at La'Nard, as he sat down next to Rebel. "Benjamin," La'Nard spoke, not expecting any verbal exchange in return.

"Don't start dad," said Rebel playfully.

Benjamin hunched his shoulders and looked from Rebel to La'Nard. "Great set," La'Nard said as he motioned for the waitress while considering this his last attempt at being cordial towards Benjamin.

"Thanks, man," said Benjamin nonchalantly.

Rebel studied the two men and thought, *this is not going to be easy*. The three of them sat uncomfortably silent for what seemed like forever, until Rebel broke the silence. "So, I scheduled this meet up with you both to discuss some serious, but happy news."

"Speak on it, Baby-girl," said Benjamin.

"I knew something was up," said La'Nard.

"I went to the doctor today, and well guys...I'm pregnant?" she said. The news was delivered more like a question than a statement.

"Pregnant?" Both La'Nard and Benjamin asked simultaneously.

"Surprise!" Rebel said.

"Yes, it's one hell of a surprise Baby-girl. I just knew you were going to say you were leaving him," said Benjamin as he looked at La'Nard.

La'Nard gave Benjamin a death stare before speaking. "Rebel may I speak with you alone?"

"Whatever you have to say to me, you can say in front of my dad. And whatever you two have against each other ends today. We're a growing family now. It's all about the baby," Rebel sternly said.

Benjamin looked at Rebel with pride. At that moment, his late wife, Rebel's mom, came to mind. She would be so excited about having a grandchild. Though they had their ups and downs, she was all about family.

La'Nard drank the contents of his glass in one, deep, gulp. He quickly stood up, causing the chair to fall over. Grabbing his jacket from the floor, he said goodbye, and walked away. Rebel ran after La'Nard, and Benjamin ran after Rebel.

"La'Nard please come back, let's discuss this," Rebel cried.

"You better wipe your face. Let his ass go. I told you he wasn't shit!" Benjamin spat.

"Daddy please," Rebel cried.

"La'Nard!" Rebel screamed. A few people turned in their seats, wondering the purpose of all the commotion.

La'Nard abruptly stopped and turned around, causing Rebel to run into him.

"What Rebel?" La'Nard shouted.

"Watch how you talk to my Baby-girl," Benjamin said in a threatening tone.

"Your Baby-girl ain't shit but a liar and a heaux," said La'Nard through gritted teeth.

Rebel was shocked at La'Nards' accusations. "What? Where is this coming from La'Nard?"

Before La'Nard could respond, Benjamin punched him in the jaw. "I told you to watch how you talk to my Baby-girl."

La'Nard shook off the pain from the punch, then stepped closer to Rebel. Benjamin pulled Rebel closer to his side. Rebel was crying hysterically.

La'Nard stepped even closer to them. "Like I said, your Baby-girl ain't shit, but a liar and a heaux. If she is pregnant, the baby ain't mine."

"La'Nard, why are you doing this? We've been together for a year. I thought you loved me," Rebel said through sobs.

Benjamin tried his best to sooth Rebel. As he looked around the restaurant, he felt shame for his daughter.

"Let me tell you why I'm doing this. I was in a horrific car accident when I was a teenager. The doctors told me I would always walk with a limp, and I would never be able to have children. Now, unless you have miracle pussy, I suggest you take your news to the other dude you were fucking."
The restaurant patrons were so quiet you could hear a pin drop. Rebel stopped crying as Benjamin stepped away from her.

"What's wrong daddy?"

"You're just like your mama. This is unbelievable," Benjamin said, throwing his hands up.

Rebel looked confused and embarrassed.

"Your mama, did the same thing to me, with you. I'm not your biological father Rebel."

Gasps could be heard throughout the restaurant. La'Nard ran his hand down his face in shock.

"This isn't the time for jokes," Rebel said angrily.

"I'm not joking. Your mom was with another man before you were born. Like La'Nard, I was in a bad car accident and became sterile. Because I loved your mother so much, I decided to forgive her and stay to help raise you. My love for you both, prevented me from ever telling you the truth. I didn't want to hurt you." Benjamin could barely stand to tell the story.

"Ain't this some shit," said La'Nard.

"I'm not my mother," Rebel shouted.

"And I'm not your baby's daddy," said La'Nard, before turning to walk away.

Rebel sat in a chair and sobbed. She couldn't believe all that transpired. What seemed like good news, turned out to be one of the worse days of her life. She turned to look at her dad, but he couldn't bear to look at her.

Removing her phone from her purse, she said, "Hey Siri, call the other one."

"Hello?" A deep male voice answered.

"Hey, Devin! I have some news for you. Can you pick me up at The Weekend?" Rebel excitedly said.

Oops! I knew it was one of them. ~VB

Be Fruitful

"And the church said amen," Pastor Shelton said as he looked around the congregation. On cue, the Ushers stood in the aisles with offering baskets.

"Great sermon, Pastor Shelton," said Lia as she shook his hand. He pulled her in for a hug that lasted way longer than necessary.

Deacon James cleared his throat, causing Pastor Shelton to let go of Lia's waist. "Lia, your mother and the baby are waiting for us by the car," said Deacon James with a stern voice.

Feeling fed up being treated like a child, Lia rolled her eyes at Deacon James before storming off towards the car.

"What is it now child?" Mrs. James asked Lia.

"Ask your husband," Lia said as she took her baby out of her mom's arms.

"You'll show some respect when you address your father," Mrs. James sternly said in a low voice.

Before Lia could respond, Deacon James walked up, ordering them to get in the car. "We will discuss your actions when we get home, Lia."

"There's nothing to discuss! I'm not a little girl anymore. If y'all can't start treating me like the woman I've become, then maybe I don't need to be around y'all," Lia cried.

"You sound childish," said Mrs. James as she shifted in her seat to look Lia in the eyes.

"Ladies, I said we will discuss this when we get home!" Deacon James shouted.

Deacon James pulled into the garage and turned the car off. Taking his thumb and pointer finger, he squeezed the bridge of his nose. "Go ahead in the house, I'll be in shortly," he said.

Mrs. James was perplexed, but did as her husband asked. Lia was halfway in the house by the time her mom got out of the car.

Deacon James got out of the car and walked over to the old tool cabinet in the corner of the garage. He reached behind an old box and pulled out a fifth of whiskey and an empty glass. Pouring himself a drink, he took a deep breath, whispering amen before downing the contents of the glass.

Walking in the house, Deacon James could hear his wife and daughter arguing. He was grateful for his stash of whiskey that calmed him during times like this.

"Lia, if you weren't so irresponsible, we wouldn't have to treat you like a child. You're only eighteen, with a baby, no husband, and no idea where the father is," Mrs. James cried.

"Daddy you're going to let her talk to me like this?" Lia whined.

"She's right you know. Who and where is this baby's father?" Deacon James questioned.

"What does he have to do with this?" Lia said.

"He has everything to do with this. My grandchild is six months old and has yet to see his father," Mrs. James spat.

Lia's phone chimed, signaling a text message had come through. Her parents continued to fuss over the baby and whatever else they could come up with while she focused on the picture message on her phone. A picture of her son's father with another woman, holding a baby around the same age as her own son, appeared from an unknown number.

"Lia, are you listening?" Mrs. James asked.

"I'll be back," said Lia as she stormed out of the house.

"Lia!" Deacon James shouted to no avail.

Lia walked five blocks to her son's, father's house. Standing across the street with her hands on her hips, she grabbed her phone from her purse and took a selfie, using his home as the background and sent it to him.

Lia's phone immediately rang.

"What are you doing here?" A low deep voice questioned.

"Come outside and see. Or do you want me to come in?" Lia said sarcastically.

"You know I can't do that, Lia. Please, go home and give me an hour to come to you," the low deep voice said.

Lia smacked her lips as she turned to walk away. Her steps were slow and intense. She wanted what she was promised from this man, a life of love and luxury. *But how can I get any of these things from a married man?* Lia thought.

As she reached her front door, the smell of Sunday dinner was in the air. Her mom's food always brought comfort to her soul.

"Where have you been?" asked Mrs. James.

"I went to see my baby's father," Lia snapped.

"Your baby's father? Where? Who is he?" Deacon James spat.

"Lia, you have to stop this nonsense. Why do you only see this man without the baby? Is there doubt in him, that he's the father?" Deacon James continued.

Lia stood there, feeling angry at her parent's accusations, and guilty, because of her own actions. She decided not to entertain their words. Instead, she sat at the table next to her son and began eating. Suddenly, Lia lost her appetite thinking about the text message she received earlier. Then, she picked up her son and went to her room.

Waiting for his father to show up, three hours had past and there was no text, phone call, or anything. Lia was devastated. However, she wasn't surprised. She cried herself to sleep that night, vowing that would be the last night she denied her son from seeing his other family.

The week went by quickly. Lia stayed home all week with her son and focused solely on him. Her parents were elated with the sudden change in her demeanor.

"Lia, I bought you and the baby new clothes for Sunday," said Mrs. James as she entered Lia's room.

"Oh, thank you, Mama. That dress is beautiful for Sunday service," said Lia.

"Lia sweetie, is there anything you need to talk about," Mrs. James asked concerned.

Lia wanted to tell her mom all about her troubles, however she couldn't bring herself to do it. "Everything's fine, Mama. I need to rest my voice for my solo tomorrow, I'll see you in the morning." Mrs. James hugged Lia and her grandson, then left the room.

It was first Sunday in June. The sun was shining and the weather was calm. The church parking lot was full. Everyone was dressed in their finest attire, ready to make a statement. Every first Sunday the aisles became a red-carpet runway. Even First Lady Shelton was showing out with her five-inch heels.

Lia took her place in the front row of the choir, amongst the sea of other royal blue robes. The choir's uniforms were a sight to behold.

Pastor and First Lady Shelton were ushered to their seats, greeting the congregation as they walked by each pew. Once they were seated, the choir director gave the signal for the choir to stand. He smiled at Lia, and on cue she took her place at the microphone just to the left of Pastor and First Lady. As the music began to play, the choir began to sway. Like clockwork, the mothers of the church began to shout, and so did the congregation as they clapped and shouted praises.

Lia worked hard on this song for two weeks. She held her hand high in the air with her eyes closed. A sound so sweet and clear traveled from the pits of her small frame, and effortlessly left her full lips:

You're a liar, and a cheat, the enemy of all things good, you sold me a dream of love and luxury, but you reneged on your promise, there is no goodness in you, you fathered my child and never paid him no mind. Hell is the set you claim, everybody from here to Jerusalem will know your dirty name...Pastor Shelton, is his dirty name!

Lia turned to look at Pastor Shelton, just as the minister of music cut the music. Just as First Lady Shelton fainted in her five-inch heels. Just as all the mothers of the church began screaming, "Deacon James get your daughter!" Just as two other young women stood and began making their way to the front of the church with multiple children each.

Pastor Shelton left First Lady Shelton on the floor as the ushers tended to her. He walked towards the podium and addressed the congregation.

"Let us pray."

"Ain't no praying, Pastor, you better start explaining yourself right now!" Deacon James yelled as he took his suit jacket off and rolled up his sleeves.

The congregation went wild egging the situation on.

"Kick his ass, Deacon James!"

"Everybody knows Pastor Shelton ain't no good."

"Look at those innocent children, looking just like Pastor."

Mrs. James sat rocking back and forth. She couldn't believe what Lia had started, though she had a feeling that her grandson was, in fact, Pastor's son. The resemblance was uncanny. The way he looked at Lia on Sundays after service, and the long unnecessary hugs, told it all.

Deacon James snatched Pastor Shelton by his leg from the pulpit. Two other deacons came and pulled him away. First Lady Shelton gained consciousness and began to cry. Just like Mrs. James, she knew all of this to be true. But Pastor was her husband, and she refused to abandon him. She loved him and prayed one day he would change.

Lia, the other two ladies, and all of their children headed down the aisle toward the exit of the church. Pastor Shelton broke away from Deacon James. Huffing and puffing, he grabbed the microphone and shouted, "Why Lia, why?"

"Because our son, and his soon to be little brother or sister deserve better. We all do," Lia said, gently placing her hand on her stomach and gesturing towards the other ladies.

First Lady Shelton fainted again. Mrs. James grabbed her purse, hooked her arm in Deacon James arm and left. Before walking out the church doors, Lia turned around and sang loudly, "See you in court Pastor. Now go pray on that."

Hell has no fury like Generation Z. They keep receipts! Here come the memes and social media. Lmao at "Hell is the set you claim."
~VB

...The End

Acknowledgments

Thank you for purchasing my book! I hope you enjoyed this collection of short stories. Kindly leave a review on the platform you used to make your purchase or feel free to share your thoughts on my Facebook or Instagram page.

Facebook: Author Honey Thomas
Instagram: Author.HoneyThomas

About the Author

"And one day she decided to pick up a pen and write"
-Honey Thomas

Honey Thomas is a Chicago, Illinois native. She is an avid reader of urban fiction novels which inspired her to write her first book. Her extensive reading of books, short stories, and poems from high school to the present day opened her mind to a world of fascination, mystery, realities, and suspense. Being an author allows her to share her creative mind with the world in hopes of giving others the same sense of escapism she experienced. Honey is currently working on her next best-sellers.

Other written works by the author:

Adult Books:

Check Mate Bitch (2 book series)

Confusion

Sunny With a Chance of Rain

Children's Books:

Just Because I'm Little Doesn't Mean I Can't Do It

The Girl with the Magical Shoes

Twin Brothers Are Cool

Ryan and the Big Math Quiz